I Need All of It

I Need All of It

Petra Postert

Illustrated by Jens Rassmus

Translated by Henriette Schroeder

FEIWEL AND FRIENDS
NEW YORK

A FEIWEL AND FRIENDS BOOK
An imprint of Macmillan Publishing Group, LLC
175 Fifth Avenue, New York, NY 10010

I NEED ALL OF IT. Text by Petra Postert. Illustrations by Jens Rassmus. © Tulipan Verlag 2015
All rights reserved.
Printed in China by RR Donnelley Asia Printing Solutions Ltd., Dongguan City, Guangdong Province.

Our books may be purchased in bulk for promotional, educational, or business use.
Please contact your local bookseller or the Macmillan Corporate and Premium Sales Department
 at (800) 221-7945 ext. 5442 or by e-mail at MacmillanSpecialMarkets@macmillan.com.

Library of Congress Cataloging-in-Publication Data is available.
ISBN 978-1-250-11271-2

Book design by Gene Vosough
Feiwel and Friends logo designed by Filomena Tuosto
Originally published under the title *Das brauch ich alles noch!*
© Tulipan Verlag GmbH München, 2015

First U.S. edition, 2018
The art for this book was created digitally.
1 3 5 7 9 10 8 6 4 2
mackids.com

For Reiner

Today is laundry day, once again.

And Jim wants to help with sorting, as usual.

Like a traffic cop, Dad stands in the middle of the laundry to show Jim what's supposed to go where.

"The white clothes to the left. Cotton. Hot cycle."

"Yes, yes," says Jim. He's heard it a hundred times.

"And the colors to the right. Cool cycle," Dad says.

"Sure."

"And all the dark stuff in the middle. Also cool cycle."

"Mmmm."

"My dark socks need extra care, of course. Over here in the basket. Warm cycle."

"Your socks are smelly socks," says Jim.

"Sorting laundry is tiring," says Dad. He pulls his hand out of Jim's trouser pocket and opens it. A stone, a key, and a button lie in his palm. Sand trickles through Dad's fingers.

"Stop!" screams Jim. "Don't throw anything away!"

"But all this can be thrown out," says Dad.

"No!" exclaims Jim. "I need all of it."

The key is twisted and rather rusty.

"You can't use it anymore," says Dad.

"The key is for a suitcase," Jim whispers. "For a large suitcase. As large as a cupboard. Made entirely of metal. And it's on rollers."

"Surely it's filled to the brim with money," says Dad.

"You have no idea," Jim says. "The suitcase belongs to a magician. Magic wand. Magic scarves. Those kinds of things are in there. And—"

"And a rabbit and two doves," interrupts Dad.

"Are you crazy? They'd starve!"

"Let the magician feed them," Dad says.

"How can he if he doesn't have a key?" asks Jim.

"Let him conjure some food. I hope a magician can perform such magic."

"He can't. Not without a book of wizardry. That's also in the suitcase. Together with all the magical spells," explains Jim.

"Poor magician," Dad says.

"Not at all!" says Jim. "He's a nasty magician."

"Oh, I see."

"He conjured a hole into the swimming pool."

"The nerve!"

"And a knot into the tail of the dachshund."

"Ouch!"

"And toads into the throat of the opera singer. And—"

"Jim, enough is enough." Dad makes a face.
"Great that we have the key now, though,"
Jim says as he grabs it and quickly shoves it
into his pocket.

"And what about this button?" Dad asks. He turns
and touches it as if it were a gemstone.
   "That's a button from a captain's jacket," Jim says.
"You can tell by the anchor."

"He must have traveled far."
"Three times around the world.
Storm and waves," Jim hollers.
"The waves as high as skyscrapers!"

"Were there palm-lined beaches and pineapples?" asks Dad.

"It was no vacation, Dad! Compass. Jungle. Tarantulas!"
Jim shrieks. "Just imagine, the captain got the button
entangled in the spider's web."

"He cursed and wriggled around and quickly cut off the button with his pocketknife. And then he ran to the ship and sailed away."

"And the button?" asks Dad.

"First it stayed in the spider's web," Jim says. "But eventually, a jungle explorer passed through by chance, removed it from the web, and pocketed it. And then lost it right away."

"And then you found it," says Dad.

"First someone else found it," Jim says. "And lost it. And then the same thing happened all over again: Found . . ."

"Lost," Dad says.

"And so on and so on. For years. Until yesterday. That's when I found it."

"Sailor's yarn!" Dad says.

"Land ho!" Jim shouts as he grabs the button and shoves it into his pocket.

Now only the stone is left in Dad's hand.

"What about this?" he asks. "It's quite a chunk."

"It's the top of a mountain!" says Jim.

"Oh, a mountain peak!"

"Once the mountain had an altitude of 16,404 feet," Jim says.

"No kidding!" says Dad.

"When I found the mountaintop, it was still covered with snow. But it melted in my pants pocket."

Dad is stunned.

"A giant bit off the mountaintop," Jim says. "He was furious.
The giant had already ripped out all the trees he could find.
And so he went high up on the mountain, took the top between
his teeth, and—*snap*—it came off. He hurled it away. And—
zoom—it fell right in front of my feet."

"Now, without a peak, the mountain must look rather odd," Dad says.

"Like a volcano," Jim says. "And if it practices long enough, at some point it will spit fire."

Jim grabs the stone and quickly shoves it into his pocket.

Suddenly Jim doesn't feel like sorting laundry anymore.

"I'll see you later, Dad," he says, already at the door.

"Look what I've found!" Dad calls. "What can this possibly be?"

"Don't you know?" asks Jim.

"Well, you tell me."

"That . . . is . . . a . . . paper clip," Jim says.

"And what else?" Dad asks.

"Nothing else," Jim says. "A paper clip. Nothing but a paper clip."